Samuel French Acting Ed

MW00625294

Log Cabin

by Jordan Harrison

SAMUELFRENCH.COM   SAMUELFRENCH.CO.UK

FOR PRODUCTION ENQUIRIES

UNITED STATES AND CANADA
Info@SamuelFrench.com
1-866-598-8449

UNITED KINGDOM AND EUROPE
Plays@SamuelFrench.co.uk
020-7255-4302

Each title is subject to availability from Samuel French, depending upon country of performance. Please be aware that *LOG CABIN* may not be licensed by Samuel French in your territory. Professional and amateur producers should contact the nearest Samuel French office or licensing partner to verify availability.

MUSIC USE NOTE

Licensees are solely responsible for obtaining formal written permission from copyright owners to use copyrighted music in the performance of this play and are strongly cautioned to do so. If no such permission is obtained by the licensee, then the licensee must use only original music that the licensee owns and controls. Licensees are solely responsible and liable for all music clearances and shall indemnify the copyright owners of the play(s) and their licensing agent, Samuel French, against any costs, expenses, losses and liabilities arising from the use of music by licensees. Please contact the appropriate music licensing authority in your territory for the rights to any incidental music.

IMPORTANT BILLING AND CREDIT REQUIREMENTS

If you have obtained performance rights to this title, please refer to your licensing agreement for important billing and credit requirements.

LOG CABIN had its world premiere at Playwrights Horizons in New York, New York on June 1, 2018. The production was directed by Pam MacKinnon, with sets by Allen Moyer, costumes by Jessica Pabst, lights by Russell H. Champa, and sound by Leah Gelpe. The production stage manager was Amanda Spooner. The cast was as follows:

EZRA	Jesse Tyler Ferguson
CHRIS	Phillip James Brannon
JULES	Dolly Wells
PAM	Cindy Cheung
HENRY	Ian Harvie
MYNA	Talene Monahon

CHARACTERS

EZRA. Late 30s, white.
CHRIS, his husband. Mid 30s, black.

JULES. Short for Julia. Late 30s.
PAM, her wife. 40.

HENRY. Late 30s, trans male.
MYNA, his girlfriend. Mid 20s.

SETTING

Jules and Pam's Brooklyn apartment, chiefly,
and a couple other lightly sketched locations.

TIME

2012 to 2017.
It may be helpful to project dates above the stage.

STYLE NOTES

Slashes (/) indicate overlapping speech.
The omission of a period indicates rolling momentum,
quick cue pick-up.

CASTING NOTES

The secondary roles are doubled as follows:
The role of **JULES'S BABY** is played by the actor who plays Henry.
The role of **HENRY'S BABY** is played by the actor who plays Chris.
The role of **HENRY** must be played by a transmasculine actor.
The role of **JULES** was written with an English accent in mind.
It isn't essential, but it has a way of making her lines sing.

PRODUCTION NOTE

To understand the characters in *Log Cabin*, one has to remember that we're watching them in the four years leading up to the 2016 election. For the Playwrights Horizons production, Pam MacKinnon and I found it helpful to orient the audience in time, not only with the mylar balloons, but with the help of projections at the top of some scenes. I'm providing the language of those projections here in **bold**, in case your theater is interested in incorporating them.

Leading into Scene One: **2012**

Transition into Scene Four: **A short year later.**

Transition into Scene Six: **Another short year later.**

Transition into Scene Eight: **A minute later.**

Transition into Scene Eleven: **Late that night.**

Transition into Scene Twelve: **A month later.**

Transition into Scene Thirteen: **A short year later.**

Transition into Scene Fourteen: **A long year later.**

Transition into the final part of Scene Fourteen (when we snap back to Ezra and company): **That very second.**

Scene One

(2012. **EZRA** *and* **CHRIS** *are visiting their married lesbian friends,* **JULES** *and* **PAM**. *Nice place, good stuff.* **EZRA** *and* **CHRIS** *are mid-story. Fast, animated:)*

EZRA. So we wait until the first round of drinks to tell him

JULES. Of course

EZRA. Let him get a little

CHRIS. Lubricated

EZRA. Ew

CHRIS. What

EZRA. He's my father

JULES. Buzzed

EZRA. Better. So now we have our martinis, good, and I say Dad, we have some amazing news, Dad. Chris and I are getting married. We know it took us a while, but yay!

(Beat. Just as before:)

Yay!

CHRIS. And Ezra's dad just sits there

JULES. No

EZRA. Not just sits, he stares into the middle distance, as if waiting for some faraway bus to come rescue him, so I say maybe you didn't hear me, Dad. There is going to be a *wedding*. We have been in a relationship for five years, as you know, a sexual relationship – we are not wacky roommates like from *The Odd Couple* – I have purchased a ring and produced it from my pocket as a holiday surprise. We held each other and cried. Chris and I are getting married.

PAM. And?

7

CHRIS. And Ezra's dad says

EZRA. "I remember it was 1982."

JULES. What?

EZRA. "Or was it '83."

CHRIS. And we're like –

EZRA. Are we awake? Is this happening? Are we both having the same dream?

CHRIS. *(As* **EZRA***'s Dad.)* "It was '82 or '83, and at first / we thought" –

EZRA. *(Taking over the impression again.)* "At first we thought it was cancer, some kind of skin cancer. But it was only the young guys getting it, these handsome young fellas."

JULES. He's talking about AIDS?

CHRIS. Hold on it gets / better –

EZRA. "And a lot of the other doctors didn't want to even look at them because they didn't *know*, how could we know if it was transmitted" –

CHRIS. And we're thinking maybe he's trying to say

JULES. "Progress!"

CHRIS. Right

JULES. "Look how far we've come!"

EZRA. *(Still as his dad.)* "...Whether it was from skin contact or eye contact or blood or what. But finally I said yes. *(A bit self-aggrandizing:)* Yes I would see them. Even if it was some kind of, / some kind of..."

CHRIS. Here it comes

EZRA. "...*Retribution*, for their behaviors."

JULES. Wait, what?

> (**EZRA** *gives her a little nod – believe it.)*

CHRIS. And Ezra and I are like

EZRA. Pause pause pause

CHRIS. Did he just?

EZRA. He *did* just

PAM. God.

EZRA. *(Rapidly.)* And my mind is racing, like Calm down Ezra, your father is a product of his *time*, maybe he's just a little too proto-Alzheimer's to complete the narrative. Maybe he's trying to say, "Oh, the wonders I've lived to see. First god was killing them for their ass-fucking, and now they're expressing longstanding commitments, mostly legal, even if I, Ezra's father, did vote against the right of my very own son" – And then I'm like no. Sorry. I can't do this.

JULES. I you? Or I your father?

EZRA. *(Duh.)* I me.

CHRIS. And suddenly Ezra is standing up – "That's it. We're going to the airport!"

JULES. Could Ezra play himself? It would be less

CHRIS. Sure

JULES. Confusing.

EZRA. *(Obliging.)* "That's it. We're going to the airport!"

CHRIS. And I'm like Ezra it's 10 p.m., there aren't going to be any flights 'til tomorrow.

EZRA. And I'm like We can sleep at the gate, we don't have to put up with this.

CHRIS. And I'm like Except we do, because he's your father.

EZRA. Except we do not, Chris. *(Seeming to forget that they're not back in the moment:)* Because it is two thousand and TWELVE, and we know that you can't get AIDS from gay people looking at you.

> *(Beat.* **JULES** *looks at* **PAM** *like, "Are they okay?" Noticing this,* **EZRA** *remembers himself.)*

So I say, "Great to catch up, 'Dad,' good visit.
Thanks for being in our corner back in '82. Thanks for saving us from the divine comeuppance we so richly deserved" –

PAM. Probably he did save some people

EZRA. He was a dermatologist!

CHRIS. So Ezra throws a few twenties on the table, and he has me by the wrist / and

EZRA. And suddenly we're out in the parking lot, like did that just happen? Did we just leave my dad in a restaurant, on New Year's Eve?

(*A sober beat.*)

CHRIS. So yeah

PAM. Wow

CHRIS. Not how we thought this would go.

JULES. So you went to the airport

EZRA. The next plane wasn't 'til 6 a.m.

CHRIS. (*Ironic.*) If only we'd seen that coming.

EZRA. So we bought some bad rosé from the airport bar

CHRIS. They let us take the whole bottle

EZRA. (Chris flirted with the bartender.)

JULES. (*Droll.*) Chris you slut

EZRA. And we got Flamin' Hot Cheetos and *Us Weeklies*, made a little fort out of our winter coats. Little Gate 23 picnic. It wasn't so bad.

CHRIS. "Happy new year!"

(*Beat.* **JULES** *shakes her head.*)

JULES. To not be happy for your own kid's happiness. To think that would somehow *take* something from you, from the country. A wedding for your kid. The failure of empathy –

CHRIS. The world is changing too fast for people to understand.

EZRA. The world isn't changing fast *enough*. Who cares if they understand?

(*Beat.* **PAM** *raises her glass.*)

PAM. To the future. May it get here soon.

ALL. (*Cheers.*) May it get here soon.

JULES. We have news.

PAM. Honey

JULES. We have to tell *someone*.

    (Droll.) We are shopping for sperm.

EZRA. You mean

JULES. *(Did I stutter?) Sperm.*

CHRIS. That's amazing!

JULES. Big sperm, little sperm. A smorgasbord.

CHRIS. A spermasbord. *(Off their blank expressions.)* Sorry.

JULES. I want an athlete, but Pam prefers a scientist.

CHRIS. Why not both?

> (**EZRA** *is still a bit dazed.*)

EZRA. You or Pam?

JULES. Having the baby? *(Duh.)* Pam.

PAM. We thought, now that there's the money from my promotion –

JULES. Pam does it all. She is Donna Reed *and* Jimmy Stewart. I'm just here to bear witness and provide a soft soundtrack of neuroses.

CHRIS. It's amazing you guys

EZRA. It is.

> *(Beat.)*

JULES. *(To* **EZRA**.*)* We thought of asking you. For your sperm I mean / but we

EZRA. Ha

JULES. Exactly, "Ha." That's what I told Pam. With close friends, it's / too –

EZRA. Complicated, totally. Plus I shouldn't pass on this jawline.

> *(Another little beat.* **EZRA** *wishes he'd been asked.)*
>
> *(Then he raises his glass again, rescuing the energy in the room.)*

The future, am I right?

JULES. *(Droll.)* It's here. The gay takeover we've been plotting, all this time

EZRA. Now this country will face our gay gay wrath.

JULES. *(À la Bond villain.)* Bwah-ha-ha.

EZRA. Bwah-ha-ha.

PAM. *(To* JULES, *faintly disapproving.)* Honey

JULES. Everybody now

JULES, EZRA, CHRIS. Bwah-ha-ha.

Scene Two

(JULES with a very pregnant PAM, several months later. JULES lies on her back, her feet stretched across PAM's lap. A brainstorm underway. PAM nixes all of JULES's ideas, wordlessly.)

JULES. Charlie. Silas. Brandon. Braden. Brady. Brodie.

PAM. You're stuck.

JULES. I'm riffing.

> *(Beat.)*

Xander. Knut. Todrick. Lunchbox.

PAM. Like actual *names*, maybe.

JULES. David. Jonathan. Ross. *(A contender.)* Ross?

PAM. *("No.")* Like on *Friends.*

> *(Beat.)*

JULES. *You* could try, you know.

> *(PAM thinks.)*

PAM. Hartley.

JULES. *(Maybe.)* Hartley.

PAM. *(Looking down at her belly.)* Hartley.

> *(JULES sits up.)*

JULES. Fuck, you're good at this.

Scene Three

(A few months later. **CHRIS** *and* **EZRA** *are waiting for the subway.* **CHRIS** *holds a huge mylar balloon in the shape of a stork holding a bundle that says "IT'S A BOY!")*

EZRA. *(Ick.)* "Hartley"?

CHRIS. It could be worse.

EZRA. Very WASP. Very B+ average at Stuyvesant.

CHRIS. It could be another Sam or Max.

EZRA. Very handcrafted wooden toys.

CHRIS. What'll it be like?

*(**EZRA** looks at him.)*

Hanging out, with a kid?

EZRA. The same as always. Pam will put out some sort of interesting cracker, and the quince paste she got last Christmas

CHRIS. *(Totally.)* Quince paste

EZRA. And that will qualify as a "spread," and we'll poke at it a little

CHRIS. The spread or the baby?

EZRA. First one, then the other. And I'll drink too much

CHRIS. *(Yes.)* Well

EZRA. And you'll pretend you're not drinking, 'til you break down and have like a *box* of wine

CHRIS. Boxed wine has come a long way

EZRA. And one of us will ask Jules about her thesis, and we'll all pretend like she's ever going to write it.

CHRIS. It's like I'm there.

EZRA. And Pam will be silent through all of this.

CHRIS. *(Charitably.)* Not *silent*, but

EZRA. Monosyllables. Wise monosyllables.

*(**CHRIS** looks up at the balloon for the first time.)*

CHRIS. That was a coup.

EZRA. Yeah.

CHRIS. You don't think it's too –

EZRA. No, it's a coup.

CHRIS. Sidebar, it's sort of lame they made us get decorations / for their

EZRA. <u>So</u> lame

CHRIS. ...Own freaking shower. As if other people don't have their own –

EZRA. Totally.

> *(Beat.)*

I mean to be fair, there's the whole pregnancy-complications thing

CHRIS. Fair

EZRA. She's been on bed rest for what

CHRIS. *(Boring.)* Months

EZRA. But Jules said it was only like twenty hours, on the day. It took me like *forty* hours to come out.

CHRIS. I bet your mom loved to remind you that.

EZRA. Whenever I was bad.

> *(Beat.)*

(Sigh.) What would Keith Haring think?

CHRIS. About?

EZRA. Or, like, David Wojnarowicz

CHRIS. I don't know who that is

EZRA. All those radical '80s art queers, if they could see us lining up for gender-coded balloons at Party fucking City. Or registering at West Elm

CHRIS. *You* picked West Elm

EZRA. *(Shrug.)* It's the best for flatware.

> *(Little beat.)*

CHRIS. It *is* pretty exciting though.

(He looks at the balloon. Suddenly sweet, childlike.)

CHRIS. Someone to care about besides ourselves. *More* than ourselves. A nephew to spoil. A kid changes you.

EZRA. I think we had different uncles.

(Beat.)

CHRIS. Do you think they'll be...

EZRA. Good at it?

*(**CHRIS** nods.)*

I think they'll be <u>too</u> good.

CHRIS. Yeah?

EZRA. Like they'll write *books* about it.

CHRIS. Yeah

EZRA. Like they'll write <u>the</u> book. And all the other parents will read about the seven stages of burping, or whatever, in their book, and then be afraid they're doing it wrong and end up raising tense and damaged kids, which was probably their secret aim in writing a book in the first place.

CHRIS. Sabotage.

EZRA. Yeah.

(Beat, beat. The cheerful balloon sways above their heads.)

Where the fuck is the train?

Scene Four

(*A short year later.* **EZRA** *and* **CHRIS** *are over at* **JULES** *and* **PAM***'s.* **JULES** *and* **PAM** *have a baby monitor to spy on their sleeping one year old in the next room. There is a platter with interesting crackers and quince paste.*)

(*A mylar balloon shaped like a puppy with a party hat that says "1!" on it floats in a corner of the ceiling.* **EZRA** *is in the middle of a story.*)

EZRA. And Henry had been cooking for hours

CHRIS. Hours!

EZRA. From this Yemeni, I don't know, cookbook

JULES. (*?*) Yemeni

EZRA. Or it could've been

CHRIS. Palestinian?

EZRA. At some point it's all hummus.

JULES. Sounds like a plan for peace in the Middle East. "At some point it's all hummus."

EZRA. You know I read that hummus has actually been highly politicized?

CHRIS. (*To* **EZRA.**) Get to the good part.

EZRA. (*"I beg your pardon."*) The good part

CHRIS. The part where she. Fuck, "He."

JULES. Chris.

　　　　(**JULES** *and* **EZRA** *are gleefully aghast.*)

CHRIS. Fuck, I am so / bad

EZRA. Yeah you are.

JULES. I read somewhere that pronouns are the last thing to – Did you tell me that, hon?

PAM. No.

EZRA. I read that too. Maybe in *Harper's*?

JULES. I don't read *Harper's*

CHRIS. Neither does he.

EZRA. I do! I read the factoids!

CHRIS. Pass the quince paste.

*(**PAM** passes the quince paste.)*

EZRA. Anyway, Henry has been cooking this fish for hours, this complicated fish – and he sets the plates in front of us, and it's two pieces

CHRIS. *(To **JULES**.)* Here it is

EZRA. Two pieces of fish for me and Chris, and one piece for Henry and his new girlfriend.

CHRIS. Myna

JULES. Like the? –

CHRIS. Like the bird.

EZRA. One piece each for him and Myna, two pieces for / us,

JULES. Yes we get it

EZRA. I guess 'cause we're the guests

CHRIS. And Ezra says

EZRA. "Look: two pieces for the boys and one piece for the girls."

JULES. Oh. My. God.

EZRA. "Look: one for the girls." And Henry just stares down at his piece of fish. And I mean, this is still – we still have three more hours of dinner

JULES. *(To **PAM**.)* Are you hearing this?

PAM. Yes.

EZRA. But it *happens* though, right?

JULES. *(Duh.)* Yeah

EZRA. This is someone I knew for twenty-four odd years as –

CHRIS. Totally

EZRA. Henry wasn't in the locker room with me getting towel-snapped. He wasn't at sleepaway, whatever, camp. He wasn't asking girls to slow dance out of some brainwashed sense of obligation. My brain stumbles over it because he wasn't <u>there</u>.

PAM. Where was he?

EZRA. Across the room, *accepting* slow dance invitations from the guys out of a brainwashed sense of obligation.

JULES. Did you guys ever slow dance together?

EZRA. I took her to prom.

JULES. *(Sardonic.)* The humanity.

EZRA. She brought two tabs of acid in her bra and we spent most of the night spacing out on the roof of the gym. She was light years ahead of high school.

JULES. *(Simple and perceptive.)* You loved her.

(Beat.)

EZRA. So he's Henry now, fine, easy, but am I supposed to edit all my memories and do a search-and-replace? And why would he even want me to? Helen *existed*, she was a person –

CHRIS. Probably he would say she *wasn't*, but –

EZRA. But he would be wrong. Were you not a person when you were in the closet?

(Little beat.)

I'm like the only one who misses her.

PAM. But wait, what did Henry

EZRA. Oh yeah

PAM. When the fish

CHRIS. Just – ashen.

EZRA. The night never really recovered.

(Little beat.)

JULES. You know what? I think that <u>sucks</u>.

*(**PAM** puts a cracker in her mouth.)*

I mean that's the whole thing with the trans movement. We're all *trying*, right? We're all fully interested in navigating this brave new world with them but it sometimes seems like they <u>want</u> us to get it wrong

EZRA. Totally

JULES. Like they're filling a quota of perceived transgressions, like with the RuPaul –

CHRIS. That's right

PAM. The RuPaul?

CHRIS. How they were all over him for using "tranny"

PAM. Him?

JULES. With him it's "him"

EZRA. Because he's a he

CHRIS. Just for using the word "tranny," in that sloppily produced part where the underwear guys are all greased up

JULES. So, like, the whole show

CHRIS. And RuPaul was like, "I was at Stonewall before any of you whiny bitches was even born."

JULES. Awesome

EZRA. Was he at Stonewall really?

CHRIS. Or whatever. The Limelight. Downtown clubs in the '90s.

EZRA. *(Ironic.)* Because same thing.

PAM. We should have him over.

JULES. RuPaul?

PAM. Henry, and his – the parrot girl

EZRA. Myna

PAM. Myna

JULES. *(Noncommittal.)* We should.

EZRA. If they're still together even. He has a new girlfriend every month

CHRIS. Every week

EZRA. He's like a teenage boy

CHRIS. It's the T.

PAM. It's / the?

CHRIS. Hormones

PAM. Ah

JULES. That's the other thing. Trans guys get to be ass-slapping misogynists because it's, you know, part of their *journey* – they're giving masculine privilege a test drive. And don't get me started on trans women.

PAM. Don't talk about the panel.

JULES. *(Immediately.)* We went to a panel, this feminist panel, and there was a trans woman who said that we / were –

PAM. That lesbians in general –

JULES. That lesbians generally are transphobic if they aren't attracted to her.

EZRA. That's...confident.

JULES. When did it become political to be repelled by a penis? We're *lesbians*, that's our <u>thing</u>.

PAM. She might have a vagina.

CHRIS. If she does, I bet it's <u>perfect</u>.

JULES. So we're there, at this alleged feminist haven, and there's a leggy, mansplaining blonde telling me she knows just as much as I do about being a woman. She's in my face, shouting "You <u>must</u> find me attractive!"

PAM. But honey, you said you *were* kind of attracted to her –

JULES. *(A very quick acknowledgement.)* She had nice shoulders. *(Immediately.)* The point is you never lose the masculine-entitlement thing, ever. But apparently you can acquire it. A few pills a day and Henry's an ass-slapping misogynist.

EZRA. I never said he was / ass-slapping –

JULES. Right. Sorry. I'm just competitive. I don't like you having another best friend.

EZRA. Well, you're best-best.

JULES. Good.

EZRA. Henry's, like, you know how you have friends from when you were young who might not be your friends if you met them later?

CHRIS. *("Come on.")* He's more than that.

(A rustling sound, over the baby monitor.)

JULES. *(To* **PAM.***)* Did he just?

PAM. No.

JULES. And yet he did. *(To* **CHRIS** *and* **EZRA.***)* Hartley is a highly frangible sleeper.

PAM. You're a highly frangible parent.

> *(***CHRIS** *mouths, "Frangible?" to* **EZRA.** **EZRA** *shrugs.)*

EZRA. You know what I miss? '70s moms.

JULES. Continue.

EZRA. They'd have twenty friends over every night and dump you in the rec room downstairs and *finis.* Or give you half a Quaalude to make sure you stayed in bed. Then they'd throw on a caftan and spend the rest of the night pulling strangers' keys from a big bowl. That's who raised us and we turned out all right.

JULES. Did we?

EZRA. Please, look at this place. You have a private deck, you have, like, *trivets*, you have a wife in finance making a cool mill

PAM. It is not a / million –

EZRA. As Director of Dyke Services at Charles Schwab.

PAM. *(Stone-faced.)* That's our word, not yours.

EZRA. What, "Schwab"?

PAM. You know what word.

> *(A scary beat.)*

PAM. Kidding!

EZRA. Wow. I think I shit my pants.

CHRIS. Money on Pam in a fight

JULES. *(Droll.)* Fight! Fight!

EZRA. *(To* **CHRIS.***)* Thanks, baby.

> *(We hear* **HARTLEY***'s cry – both through the monitor and from the other room.)*

JULES. Don't tell me *that* wasn't –

PAM. Just let him cry it out.

JULES. Oh sure, let our child starve, / easy

PAM. He's not starving, remember the book.

JULES. *(To* **CHRIS** *and* **EZRA.***)* "Ways and Weans: The Guide to an Autonomous Youngster."

> *(Another cry from the next room.* **JULES** *tries to be a '70s mom.* **CHRIS** *puts some cheese on a cracker.)*

CHRIS. This cheese is bananas.

PAM. Is that a good thing?

JULES. It's Muenster.

CHRIS. *("Who knew.")* Muenster.

> *(Beat.)*

JULES. I'm gonna just –

> *(***JULES** *rushes off.)*

PAM. Yeah, so that's happening.

CHRIS. I think it's sweet. I've never seen her be, you know, maternal.

PAM. Do you guys ever talk about...?

EZRA. *(Quickly.)* No.

CHRIS. Well

EZRA. <u>No</u>.

Scene Five

(In the next room, **JULES** *talks to her* **BABY**, *played by a large grown man. The other end of the baby monitor lies nearby.* **JULES'S BABY** *doesn't act like a kid. He's just a placid, hairy, matter-of-fact adult surrounded by some expensive-looking plush animals and handcrafted wooden toys.)*

JULES. I heard you crying.

BABY. Was I.

JULES. It was right there in the monitor.

BABY. *(Matter-of-fact.)* The monitor doesn't lie.

JULES. Why were you crying?

BABY. I was either sad or I was hungry. Or confused. I mean you just...took off.

JULES. I told you, I'm in the next room with friends.

BABY. Oh yes.

JULES. Right there in the next room.

BABY. What do you talk about, you and your friends?

JULES. Adult things. You'd be bored. Sometimes *I'm* bored.

BABY. *(Vaguely hopeful.)* Are there animals there?

JULES. Not usually. *(Beat.)* Do you want me to tell you a story, to help you get back to sleep?

BABY. If you like.

JULES. How about the one with the baby dinosaurs?

BABY. *(Faintly condescending.)* You do like that one.

JULES. Or the one with the young prince and the sleeping potion.

BABY. It's a little schematic, don't you think? You could bury the bedtime message better.

JULES. All right, I get it. You want a new story.

BABY. It's time, don't you think?

JULES. *(To herself.)* The pressure of a new story...

Okay. There was once a girl with long brown hair

BABY. Was she a princess?

JULES. She was not.

BABY. Was she an animal?

JULES. No. She was just an ordinary little girl with long brown hair, who liked other little girls and was sometimes afraid to go outside.

BABY. *(Aha.)* She was a lesbian.

JULES. Well, yes. And she grew up and met another grown-up little girl, another lesbian. And they got married.

BABY. And happy ever after?

JULES. Not yet.

> *(Lights snap back to* **PAM**, **EZRA**, *and* **CHRIS** *in the living room. Instead of the conversation we've just been watching, we hear the sound of an actual one year old through the monitor, gurgling innocuously.)*

CHRIS. Muenster is German?

PAM. *(Apologetic.)* American, I think.

JULES. *(Baby talk, through the monitor.)* Woodja woodja woodja.

> *(The* **BABY** *gurgles.)*

CHRIS. But then why is it called –

EZRA. So they can charge more.

CHRIS. Who's "they"? The evil American cheese council?

> *(Lights snap back to* **JULES** *and the* **BABY**.*)*

JULES. So after a couple of years of mere happiness, this woman, her wife, talked her into having a child, because by then it was the thing to do.

BABY. What do you mean the thing to do?

JULES. Well. They couldn't get married, and then they could. Their families wouldn't accept them, and then they would. They didn't have any money, and then they did. There had to be something else to want. So, a baby.

BABY. Is this a true story?

JULES. All good stories have an element of truth.

BABY. I'm not sure I agree, but go on.

JULES. So this baby came along, after a fair amount of medical intrigue and intervention, and they loved it mostly.

BABY. Mostly?

JULES. Well, the thought of a boy was never not terrifying, of course. He was another species. And she worried that he still wasn't talking. Her friends looked at her funny, like she must've dropped him. Like she hadn't read to him in utero, or played Mozart.

BABY. It's fairly common to be preverbal at twelve months.

JULES. She had whole imaginary conversations with him, to fill the silence. But she found that he was rarely her *ally* in these conversations.

BABY. *(Not quite assuaging.)* I'm sorry you feel that way.

JULES. She found herself thinking: even though he doesn't talk yet, he listens. He sees. He sees what is rotten in me. He sees what I've done. He knows the things I want, the things I don't even admit to myself, in the dark hours, much less to his other mom.

> *(A knock on the door and **PAM** enters, not waiting for an answer.)*

PAM. Everything okay?

JULES. Of course.

PAM. You've been in here for half an hour. The boys are getting restless.

JULES. The boys are always restless.

> *(To the **BABY**.)* Look who came to visit, Baby! It's your mom!

PAM. Hello, Baby!

> *(The **BABY** waves hello.)*

(Lights snap back to **CHRIS** *and* **EZRA** *in the living room, nibbling on the sad remnants of Muenster and quince paste. Through the monitor, we hear.)*

PAM. *(Voice only.)* Who's a good baby? Who's a good baby?

(Sound of one year old gurglings.)

EZRA. *(Not cute.)* Cute.

(Beat.)

CHRIS. Can you believe she asked?

EZRA. *(Shrug.)* It's the thing to ask gay people now. After "Are you getting married?"

CHRIS. Jules seems crazy.

EZRA. Jules is always crazy.

CHRIS. *(Dry.)* But there's a new depth to her work.

EZRA. Yeah, well. That's what kids do to you.

(A happy gurgle from the monitor.)

CHRIS. If you ever want to talk about it more...

EZRA. We've talked about it.

(Beat.)

EZRA. *("I was right.")* Quince paste.

Scene Six

(A short year later. **PAM** *and* **JULES**'s *place. There is a new mylar balloon, shaped like Thomas the Train Engine, in a corner of the apartment. It has the words "Choo choo, you're TWO!" on it.)*

JULES. *(To* **EZRA** *and* **CHRIS**, *mid-conversation.)* I give it a year tops –

> *(***PAM*** *calls from the kitchen, where she's putting finishing touches on the cheese plate.)*

PAM. Baby you promised –

JULES. He's not here yet, I'm getting it out of my system!

PAM. One night of small talk.

JULES. *(Back to* **EZRA** *and* **CHRIS**.*)* Maybe it'll take a little longer because people are afraid –

CHRIS. Afraid?

JULES. To set the movement back

EZRA. Right

PAM. *(To herself, a futile example of small talk.)* "Seen any good movies lately?"

EZRA. *(To* **JULES**.*)* And to give up all that good will

JULES. But at some point, a trans person will say, "I made a mistake. I was so sure. I thought I was a woman born in a man's body"

EZRA. Or / a man in a woman's –

JULES. "But I gave it a try, and it turns out I do not like being a woman AT ALL. It turns out it is a giant BUMMER. I don't like my breasts, they hurt my back. I don't like my little nub in place of a majestic penis" –

CHRIS. *(Amused and grossed out.)* "Nub"

JULES. "But most of all I miss my God-given privilege, my patriarchal *je ne sais quoi*, and I want it back. Sorry everyone. Never mind."

PAM. A lot of them don't get bottom surgery, honey.

JULES. Do you think Henry...?

EZRA. *(Shrug.)* Don't look at me.

CHRIS. Trans people hate that question.

EZRA. Yeah, but why?

PAM. Do they ask you about your genitalia?

EZRA. They don't have to. They've heard the legends.

(**JULES** *rolls her eyes.*)

CHRIS. Did we have that with gay marriage?

JULES. *(Non sequitur.)* Did we have what with gay marriage?

CHRIS. "Oops, we fought for all this, tooth and nail – our gay forefathers, Larry Kramer, whoever, fought for this – for this right – but now we're getting a divorce. Sorry everyone, gay people fall out of love too."

EZRA. *(Valiant.)* Never!

(**JULES** *glances up at the mylar balloon.*)

JULES. Thanks for doing that.

EZRA. *(It wasn't nothing.)* Oh it's nothing. It's like tradition now. Muscling past the moms at Party City.

CHRIS. Is he talking yet?

EZRA. Chris

CHRIS. What?

PAM. It's okay. He's not. He's experimenting with multisyllable sounds, which the pediatrician says is encouraging, but.

EZRA. It'll happen.

JULES. *(Stressed but covering.)* Two years old. He was supposed to be exceptional, and now he's on the wrong side of exceptional

EZRA. It'll happen.

JULES. *(To **PAM**.)* You didn't, like, fuck the mail lady while he was watching, did you? In his formative months?

PAM. She's kidding.

JULES. Pam *luuuurves* the mail lady. They talk for hours

PAM. She's like sixty.

JULES. A silver fox.

EZRA. Isn't that just men?

JULES. A silver sable.

EZRA. I'll allow it.

> (*Little beat.* **CHRIS** *looks toward the door to* **HARTLEY**'s *room.*)

CHRIS. You think he'll come say hi later?
Or not *say*, but

JULES. He's shy.

CHRIS. We're his uncles!

EZRA. We're not, but

JULES. (*Kindly decisive.*) You are.

EZRA. I think I was shyer of my uncle than anyone in the world.

CHRIS. (*To* **PAM**, *by way of an explanation.*) He was in Nam.

EZRA. Very into protocol. Very Captain Von Trapp.

CHRIS. (*"Yum."*) Captain Von Trapp.

EZRA. Really?

CHRIS. (*À la sexual role play.*) "Aye aye, Captain."

EZRA. Should we add that to our repertoire?

JULES. Ew.

EZRA. Don't "ew" to our repertoire! Don't you guys have a repertoire?

JULES. (*Dry.*) No, we are sufficient for each other.

CHRIS. You never think about other people?

EZRA. (*To* **CHRIS**, *mock-offended.*) You think about other people?

CHRIS. I mean, sure. But then I ask you to play them.

EZRA. (*To* **JULES** *and* **PAM**.) I contain multitudes.

JULES. I repeat: Ew.

CHRIS. Besides, they're mostly fictional, my fantasy guys.

JULES. "Mostly."

(The door buzzer buzzes.)

EZRA. That'll be him.

CHRIS. *(Reinforcing this.)* "Him."

EZRA. All together now

CHRIS, JULES & EZRA. Him.

PAM. *(Disapproving.)* Guys.

*(**PAM** goes for the door.)*

EZRA. We should talk about something else or he'll know.

JULES. If only we cared for sport.

EZRA. "Sports," Jules, / they're called sports.

JULES. I know, I'm joking!

CHRIS. Quick, think.

*(But **PAM** is already opening the door.)*

PAM. Henry!

HENRY. *(Folksy.)* Hello, hello.

*(**HENRY**, their trans male friend is there with his very young, very pretty – in a patchouli-scented, Oberlin dropout way – girlfriend, **MYNA**. They have a wrapped present.)*

MYNA. Oh my god, this place is amazing.

Scene Seven

(A few minutes later. **HENRY** *has settled into the couch with the others.* **MYNA** *looks around, admiring tchotchkes.)*

HENRY. What they do is they send you a little manila envelope

MYNA. In the mail

JULES. *(To* **EZRA**, *fake-helpfully.)* In the mail

EZRA. Shh

HENRY. And there's nothing in it but a map, on like vellum

EZRA. Hipster nonsense

HENRY. Um, yeah. And you get there and it's B.F. Nowhere, and you're like "Is this it?" because there's only a, like a –

MYNA. Lemonade stand from hell.

HENRY. Lemonade stand from hell. This brown little wooden shack with a boarded-up window, right on the edge of the canyon wall. And you knock on the little window, and it slides open like *The Wizard of Oz*, and this hot surly girl pokes her head out and says, "Password?" And I don't have a password, they forgot it somehow, in the envelope, so I'm like "...Open Sesame?" And this girl was like "N to the O."

CHRIS. *("I haven't heard that in ages.")* "N to the O"

HENRY. And if she had gum she'd be snapping it. And the little window goes slam, and I'm like – it's the *desert*. I drove three hours, I'm not giving up. So I knock on the little window again, and the hot mean girl says "Password?" like I wasn't just there a second ago. And what am I going to say? My computer password? My birthdate? When all of a sudden this voice behind me shouts out

MYNA. "Fruit Brute!"

JULES. *(Confused.)* "Fruit Brute"?

HENRY. *(A nod to* **EZRA**.*)* Hipster nonsense.

MYNA. *(She just likes saying it.)* Fruit Brute!

EZRA. *(To* **JULES**, *sagely.)* It was one of those '80s monster cereals, like Frankenberry only lesser

CHRIS. You see, to me it was more-er

HENRY. *("I have the conch.")* And *so*, this girl I've never even seen before slides up to me. Just as hot as the mean girl only nice

MYNA. Aww

HENRY. And she says

MYNA. "This fella's with me."

HENRY. "This fella's with me." And remember, this was a year ago. I wasn't getting "sirred" all the time, I didn't have my facial hair. "This fella's with me." So I just about creamed my jeans right there. *(Off of* **JULES***'s expression.)* What.

JULES. Oh it's – not the most *stylish* phrase

HENRY. *(Not sorry.)* Sorry, didn't know this was a family audience. So the mean girl opens the door and there's this whole other world in there, carved right into the rock wall. Like a secret city. Drum and bass and pink foam and eyebrow piercings

EZRA. Like the '90s exploded everywhere

MYNA. *(Awed and excited.)* You remember the '90s! We have to talk.

HENRY. And we danced all night, me and this stranger girl, and we limped out of the desert together at 6 a.m. and drove to a truck stop and ordered eggs over easy.

MYNA. *(Chipper.)* And we fucked in the bathroom and the eggs were waiting for us when we got back. And they were still runny.

> *(Beat.)*

PAM. It's a great story, Henry. Like something out of a rom-com.

EZRA. Twenty-first century rom-com.

HENRY. Goodbye, McAdams. So long, Gosling.

MYNA. Hello, Henry!

>   (**MYNA** *wraps her arms around him.*)

>   (*Sound of the* **BABY** *crying, over the monitor.*)

PAM. *(To* **JULES***.)* He's fine.

HENRY. Good little lungs on him

JULES. We're very proud

HENRY. Who had him, you or?

JULES. Pam did.

EZRA. Think you'll try next?

JULES. Some of us don't need to experience the joys of cervical tearing.

HENRY. I'm dying to have a kid.

CHRIS. Yeah?

HENRY. It's just something I gotta do. I mean, Myna would have it of course.

MYNA. *(Annoyed.)* "Of course."

EZRA. Doesn't *anybody* like cervical tearing?

MYNA. I'm only twenty-six, I have a lot I want to do first. I wanna travel

HENRY. You can travel with kids

MYNA. *(Intense.)* To *Tibet*? To the tree of life in *Bahrain*?

HENRY. *(To the others.)* Sorry, this is an ongoing

MYNA. Yup

HENRY. Conversation.

MYNA. *(To* **HENRY***.)* You want one so much, *you* have it.

HENRY. Mean.

JULES. You can do that?

HENRY. Technically. I mean I have a uterus. But it's not really...

>   (*He doesn't say "an option."*)

I'd have to go off the T.

EZRA. Pregnant lady with a beard.

HENRY. Pregnant guy with a beard.

EZRA. Shit. Jesus, sorry man.

HENRY. *(Lightly, with a touch of ice.)* It's okay, I'm used to it.

MYNA. *(To* **EZRA** *and* **CHRIS**.*)* And you? What about you guys? Do you...?

EZRA. Have a uterus? No.

CHRIS. It's a perfectly legitimate question.

(To **MYNA**.*)* We want to travel too, / so.

MYNA. Right?

CHRIS. Plus we have Hartley. We get to give him a hug and kiss and run off when he gets cranky.

HENRY. I'm up for the cranky part.

I'm up for all of it.

        (HENRY *takes* **MYNA***'s hand.)*

Of course, this lady comes first.

JULES. *(To* **MYNA**.*)* Now. You'll have to forgive me for being ignorant, or um, controversial –

MYNA. *("Where's this going?")* Oh

JULES. But do you always –?

Like do you *specifically* –?

MYNA. Do I always date trans guys?

JULES. Thank you, yes.

HENRY. Why is that controversial?

MYNA. Yeah.

EZRA. *(Busting her balls.)* Yeah Jules, why.

JULES. Right, good question. *(To* **EZRA**.*)* Everyone.

MYNA. I mean it isn't like a *fetish* but yeah, mostly trans guys. I dated a few cis guys too, way back in college

HENRY. Like two years ago

MYNA. *Five* years. And I've been with a few girls, but who hasn't.

        (EZRA *raises his hand, unnoticed.)*

JULES. But again, is this something you specifically desire, above other things? Because that is very specific. If

you were born a hundred years ago, you wouldn't
have been able to find a single person on the planet to
satisfy / that want.

HENRY. Not necessarily

JULES. Or would the want not have existed yet? Was the
demand created by the supply?

MYNA. This is... / a lot

PAM. *(To* **JULES.***)* Yeah, honey

JULES. Sorry, just one question then: is there something
you get from trans men that you wouldn't from, what
did you call it?

MYNA. Cis guys.

EZRA. I bet Henry knows exactly what to do, 'cause he's
been on the other end of it.

PAM. *(As in sexual?)* What to do?

EZRA. *(Yes, sexual.)* I mean he knows how to get it *done.*

MYNA. That's not *un*true.

CHRIS. But you get that with gays and lesbians too.
Familiarity with the equipment.

EZRA. We are highly familiar

MYNA. But with Henry there's a real attentiveness...

HENRY. *(To* **PAM.***)* I'm *almost* uncomfortable.

PAM. I'm there.

MYNA. ...A *giving*, I guess, that you wouldn't necessarily
have with cis guys. No offense

EZRA. None / taken –

MYNA. Combined with the whole *you're-just-mean-
enough-to-fulfill-my-unspoken-daddy-fantasies* thing
you don't get with lesbians.

JULES. I don't know, they sound pretty spoken to me

MYNA. What

JULES. The fantasies

HENRY. You don't know the half of it.

(He looks at **JULES.** **JULES** *breaks eye contact.)*

CHRIS. *(Shaking his head, almost to himself.)* "Cis" guys.

MYNA. What

CHRIS. Nothing

HENRY. No, what?

CHRIS. Really / it isn't

EZRA. It's nothing

HENRY. *(Cordial.)* No. I wanna know.

CHRIS. Um, okay. That word. "Cis" guys. It makes me feel a little

HENRY. A little…

CHRIS. I mean do you realize when you say that, you're putting us in a category?

HENRY. Yes.

CHRIS. You're putting me in a category with all the high school fucktards I had to grow up with in Wichita. The ones who played lacrosse and dated cheerleaders and dressed up in their cheerleader girlfriends' outfits on Halloween for fun, who cut class and never got caught, who called me faggot. Or nigger.

MYNA.	**PAM**.
Oh, god	Chris

JULES. *(Naively aghast.)* They really said that?

CHRIS. Uh, yeah girl.

(Back to **HENRY**.*)* You're saying I'm one of / those guys

MYNA.	**HENRY**.
No, we're not.	No.

EZRA. Well yes, actually. You're saying they're cis guys and Chris and I are cis guys and all of us got the keys to the kingdom, and I'm sorry but it didn't feel that way for the first three decades-plus of my life.

HENRY. And now it does.

EZRA.	**MYNA**.
What?	*("Steady.")* Henry.

HENRY. You said yourself: you didn't feel that way for three decades, and now / you do –

EZRA. I just mean how in the last couple years, things have gotten a little / more –

HENRY. And for me it's still three more decades of public bathroom legislation, three more decades of driving to the fucking desert to find people who are like-minded, so yeah, I think you belong in a category of people who are easier for society to accept, and there's a name for that category and it's called a "cis male."

JULES. Maybe it's the word

HENRY. What?

JULES. Maybe the problem is the word sucks.

HENRY. Nice.

JULES. Cis. I mean what does that even / mean–

MYNA. It's Latin / I think

HENRY. Cisgender. It means "on this side of," as opposed to the other / side

EZRA. Well it sounds like "siss," like S-I-S, / it sounds like sissy.

MYNA. It's C-I

EZRA. I just don't see why the trans community gets to call us something that we were scared to get called in middle school.

HENRY. *(Shrug.)* Homonyms.

EZRA. So, you get to choose what we call you *and* what you call us.

HENRY. I'll call you what I want. No one's saying you have to answer.

> (**CHRIS** *is shaking his head, still processing all this.*)

CHRIS. I'm sorry, but. You really think I have the keys to the kingdom?

HENRY. Those were Ezra's words –

CHRIS. That I have some sort of advantage, in this society, over a white trans guy?

HENRY. Maybe not *every* black cis guy, but your parents have money.

CHRIS. Oh, *now* we're / talking about

HENRY. You grew up in the biggest house in the whole state of Kansas – *(To* **EZRA**.*)* Didn't you say that?

EZRA. *One* of the biggest, maybe

CHRIS. *(To* **HENRY**.*)* So I'm not black. Because I have a trust fund and a bunch of white / friends.

HENRY. I would never / say that

EZRA. *(To* **CHRIS**.*)* He's not saying / that

HENRY. I'm just saying the challenges of someone with money and a Harvard diploma aren't the same as / someone who –

CHRIS. How does that help me when I walk into a store and the manager follows me around; when I try to get a cab. I'm a faggot in Harlem and I'm a "thug" in white Brooklyn. And you know what I am in the Wichita school district.

MYNA. *(White-guilt squirmy.)* Please don't say it.

CHRIS. What? "Wichita?"

>   *(Back to* **HENRY**.*)*

> How is any of that cis? How is that "on this side of"? No matter where I am, it's the other side of.

>   *(Pause pause pause.* **EZRA** *rubs* **CHRIS**'s *shoulder.* **CHRIS** *shakes his hand off.)*

MYNA. Um, Ezra, what are you writing these days?

EZRA. An attempt at levity – sure, we can do that. I'm not working on anything at the moment. By which I mean the last six months. It's a drought.

JULES. *("Don't say that.")* It's a lull

MYNA. Henry showed me some of your pieces, / and

EZRA. *(Kind of touched.)* He did?

MYNA. I really loved them, especially the one about gay suicide being a self-victimizing stereotype.

EZRA. I got a lot of nasty comments after that one.

MYNA. I'm totally in support of creative lulls. I think most countries understand that better than we do – the need to pause and recharge.

> *(Pause. Then another, more successful attempt at levity.)*

PAM. We have a roof garden.

MYNA. *Whaaa?*

PAM. ... If you guys wanna check it out.

JULES. We just put in a bar.

EZRA. *(Echoing* **MYNA**, *semi-affectionately.) Whaaa?*

PAM. And a grill

EZRA. *(To* **JULES**.*)* I knew the grill was coming, but a bar? Very one percent.

JULES. *You're* one percent.

EZRA. I know you are but what am I?

JULES. One percent.

> *(***HENRY*** snorts. ***JULES*** locks eyes with him again.)*

PAM. We're not totally stocked up yet, but we could make mojitos, / or

MYNA. MOJITOOOS!

EZRA. *(Snobby.)* Caipirinhas are better.

JULES. *(To* **HENRY***: "case closed.")* One percent.

MYNA. What's a Caipa – Caipa –

EZRA. Not so sugary.

MYNA. *(Shrug.)* I like sugar.

JULES. *(To* **PAM**.*)* I'll go put Hartley down.

CHRIS. "Put him down," it always sounds like euthanasia.

JULES. Don't tempt me.

PAM. Honey.

> *(***PAM**, **EZRA**, **MYNA**, *and* **CHRIS** *start to climb out the window to the adjacent roof garden.)*

MYNA. *(To* **HENRY**.*)* You coming?

HENRY. I'm actually gonna stay in here. Simmer down a little.

> *(Looking at* JULES.*)*

If that's cool.

MYNA. I'll make you a mojito.

HENRY. Beer would be great.

MYNA. *(To* JULES.*)* I forgot, I'm dating John Wayne.

Scene Eight

*(A minute later. **JULES** enters the baby's room, followed by **HENRY**. There is a little Indian tepee on the floor that presumably **HARTLEY** is sitting inside, though it is much too small for the adult actor.)*

JULES. Hartley? You asleep already, baby?

> *(To **HENRY**.)*

He likes to sleep in there now. He can sleep sitting up, the little weirdo.

HENRY. Man, I wish I had one of these when I was a kid.

JULES. Me too.

Actually I was obsessed with ponies. My secret shame.

HENRY. Ponies?

JULES. As in My Little. Lavender ponies with sparkles on their heinies. So disappointing right? What a fucking girl.

HENRY. Nothing wrong with girls.

JULES. No.

> *(This hangs in the air.)*

It's ponies I'm against.

HENRY. I had one too.

JULES. Yeah?

HENRY. "Skybright." He had a big rainbow on his ass.

JULES. That's where rainbows come from.

> *(**HENRY** chuckles politely.)*

I know. That wasn't actually *wit*. Sometimes if you deliver it well enough people can't tell. *(Mocking her own delivery.)* "That's where rainbows come from." Half of Oscar Wilde is terrible if you look at it long enough, but I imagine his delivery more than made up...

> *(She bails on this tangent.)*

JULES. Are we? Is this a?

HENRY. Is this a...

JULES. You stayed behind.

HENRY. Those guys are bugging the shit out of me.

JULES. I thought maybe you stayed behind because...

HENRY. Because?

> *(Is **HENRY** really unsure what she means? Or is he just toying with her?)*

JULES. You looked at me.

HENRY. I looked at you?

JULES. You looked at me like you could see through my clothes.

> *(He looks at her.)*

Like that, yeah.

HENRY. I come to your house, you pummel me with all these retrograde, / like, questions

JULES. Yeah, that was –

HENRY. Why would I want to fuck you?

JULES. I don't know.

> *(Beat. It's as if she's said, "I don't know, but you do.")*

I mean, I might have to let you take the *lead*, I don't have a lot of experience / with –

HENRY. *(Laughing to himself.)* Jesus.

JULES. What?

HENRY. Such a cliché. Cis girls always want to be *shown*. What if I'm bored with educating you all? Being your gateway drug? What if <u>I</u> want to get slammed against a wall, what if <u>I</u> want to get taken care of? And you're the biggest offenders – the ones who doubled down on being a lesbian but miss catching a dick in college.

JULES. *(Deadpan.)* Sorry, I didn't know my libido was a cliché.

HENRY. Well it is.

> (**HENRY** *takes a seat. Maybe he sits in a plastic kids' chair.*)

What did you think we'd do?

JULES. It's embarrassing.

HENRY. *(Bored now.)* I bet.

JULES. *(Rising to the challenge.)* You'd go down on me. Bite my nipples. Stick your fingers inside me.

HENRY. *(Dry.)* Sounds like a lot of work for me.

JULES. –

HENRY. *(A command.)* How about you start yourself off?

JULES. You mean –

> (**HENRY** *wordlessly answers, "You know what I mean." **JULES** glances at the tepee, guilty.*)

HENRY. Better hurry. They'll be back.

> (**JULES** *starts to touch herself, self-conscious.*)

That's how you do it?

JULES. Well

HENRY. Don't do it "for" me.

> (**JULES** *continues, closing her eyes. A little less perform-y.*)

(Slow, steady.) I see how this works. You need a guy in your pants every now and then, you invite a stranger over... Do you always wait for your wife to give the roof-deck tour? Or do you sometimes let her watch?

JULES. *(Under her breath.)* Call me a cliché again.

HENRY. Don't give me orders, you fucking cis girl cliché.

> (**HENRY** *stands.* **JULES** *continues.*)

You think I like being objectified by you little sex tourists? You bored housewives?

JULES. No.

HENRY. Open your legs.

Better.

You're the object.

How's it feel?

(**JULES** *comes.*)

(*The tepee rustles for a second. They freeze, but the tepee returns to rest.*)

Did I say stop?

(*Little beat.*)

JULES. You said, they'll be back.

HENRY. Not yet.

(*Continuous into:*)

Scene Nine

(**MYNA** *stands alone in the living room, white as a sheet, holding* **HENRY**'s *beer. She is completely still, arrested by what she's been hearing over the baby monitor.*)

HENRY. *(Voice only.)* We still have some time.

JULES. *(Voice only.)* I feel a little

HENRY. *(Voice only.)* What

JULES. *(Voice only.)* Selfish.

HENRY. *(Voice only.)* Okay.

JULES. *(Voice only.)* Do you want?
    Can I –

HENRY. *(Voice only.)* What, get me off?
    You already did.

JULES. *(Voice only.)* And I thought we weren't getting along.

HENRY. *(Voice only.)* Who says we're getting along?

(*We hear noise from the roof deck, the others returning.*)

PAM. *(Offstage.)* That's an actual show?

EZRA. *(Offstage.)* Uh-huh.

(**MYNA** *makes some purposeful noise. Bringing the beer down on a table, kicking a chair. A little too loud.*)

MYNA. Thanks for showing us that, Pam!

JULES. *(Over baby monitor.)* Shit. I told you. Shit.

PAM. *(Offstage.)* What's that?

MYNA. I said that was amazing!

(**PAM** *climbs in through the window from the roof deck, holding a couple of abundant-looking mojitos, one for* **JULES.**)

That big old sycamore – you should make a tire swing for Hartley!

PAM. *(Nodding toward the monitor.)* Not too loud, he's probably out by now.

MYNA. Oh. Sorry.

> *(**MYNA** looks at the monitor, freaked. But it's mercifully silent now. **CHRIS** and **EZRA** climb in from the roof deck, mojitos in hand.)*

EZRA. It's a blight I tell you.

CHRIS. That seems like / an oversta –

EZRA. *(Cheerfully outraged.)* A blight on society!

CHRIS. *(To **PAM**.)* Look what you started.

EZRA. It's the only thing Hollywood does anymore: the Wicked Witch wasn't actually Wicked, she was <u>misunderstood</u>. Captain Hook was <u>misunderstood</u>. Maleficent – I mean her name is *Maleficent*, what's not to understand?

PAM. Who cares, they're just kids' movies.

EZRA. Because, Pamela, my second-best friend, because: our kids are no longer learning that there is evil in the world. Absolute evil. Terrorist militants are not *misunderstood*. They did not become evil because it was hard growing up with green skin, or they lost their hand to a crocodile. They are driven by the will to destroy you and everyone you love.

> *(Beat.)*

CHRIS. Except, they *did* kind of have to grow up with green skin.

EZRA. You mean

CHRIS. The terrorists.

EZRA. Are we talking about race again?

CHRIS. No we are not talking about race "again," which by the way we never talk about.

> *(**JULES** and **HENRY** emerge from the bedroom. **JULES** tries not to look flushed.)*

EZRA. You just said grow up with green skin.

CHRIS. Elphaba isn't a minority, she's a metaphor.

EZRA. I can't even look at you.

HENRY. *(Taking the beer from* **MYNA**.*)* What are we talking about?

PAM. *(Grimly ironic.)* I asked if anyone had seen any good movies. *(To* **JULES**, *re: the baby.)* Is he?

JULES. Mm-hmm.

> *(**PAM** tries to hand the extra mojito to **JULES**.)*

Wait a sec. *(**JULES** goes to wash her hands in the kitchen sink.)* I had to change him.

> *(**MYNA** clocks this.)*

CHRIS. *(Still to* **EZRA**.*)* It's not that anyone's actually green, it's that they're an outsider – we're all outsiders. We're *all* the green girl.

HENRY. Seriously, what is / happening

EZRA. My husband is comparing terrorist cells to Adele Dazeem.

CHRIS. … Or we all *think* we're the green girl, whether it's because we're gay, or a nerd, or the one black kid in the whole fucking Kansas school system –

HENRY. Look, I'm sorry about earlier

EZRA. Don't worry about it.

> *(**CHRIS** glances at **EZRA** – "Don't speak for me.")*

CHRIS. I'm not looking for sorry, I just think it's a failure of empathy – not to mention a dangerous, like, America blind spot – to say that terrorists were born evil. I'm sure they had to endure a good deal of disenfranchisement, pigment-related or otherwise.

EZRA. So, you're glad that our children's entertainment is training kids to see the other side of terrorism.

CHRIS. No, I / just think –

EZRA. This country has gotten too liberal. / There. // I said it.

MYNA. *(Overlapping at "/".)* Wait, what?

CHRIS. *(Overlapping at "//".)* Let me talk!

EZRA. *(To* **CHRIS.***)* You've *been* talking. These people would kill you RIGHT NOW if they could, Chris.

CHRIS. Our *cat* would kill us right now if it could.

EZRA. And they wouldn't just shoot you. They would set your corpse on fire and parade you down the center of town with an American flag shoved in your mouth

CHRIS. Jesus, Ezra

EZRA. So excuse me if I'm not so interested in finding the multi-faceted *motivation* behind their wish to obliterate us from the face of the planet, just for being gay, or having enough to eat, or having a SodaStream or whatever imagined thing we've done wrong. God. We're all so fucking afraid of being politically incorrect. Liberalism is a kind of mass conformity.

PAM. So you'd prefer those enlightened mavericks in the Republican party, who wouldn't even give you the right to pull the plug on Chris if they had their way.

CHRIS. Who's pulling my plug now?

PAM. Not him

EZRA. Jules, help me out, you're the other bleeding-heart neo-con here.

JULES. Sorry, what was the question?

PAM. Hon? You're awfully quiet.

EZRA. Doesn't anybody know what I'm talking about?

HENRY. I do.

EZRA. You do?

HENRY. I live with an actual human being who doesn't remember not having a cell phone

MYNA. How is that / even –

HENRY. It was placed in her hands at age two instead of a pacifier

MYNA. It was not, my parents had very strict / rules –

HENRY. And her millennial friends come by, and these kids – sorry, honey – but these kids have no will of their own. They spend their lives hitting the "like" button, Like Like Like Like. Whatever cause, whatever protest anyone's doing is worthy of ecstatic support

PAM. Or ecstatic vitriol

HENRY. Yes, this. Either way the problem is the same – they've never had to build an argument for themselves. There's no moral consideration –

MYNA. Are you giving me a lesson on morals. Is that really what's happening?

HENRY. I'm speaking broadly about your generation

MYNA. And excuse me if I'm okay with Like Like Like because all I see right here is Consume Consume Consume. Consume and spit out

HENRY. Baby, you're drunk.

MYNA. I am thoroughly *not*.

HENRY. Well you're sputtering.

MYNA. Cheese plate! Rooftop bar! Moral consideration? You're not even pretending.

> *(Beat.)*

You all have *so much*. It's disgusting. Don't you find it disgusting?

What are you contributing? Who are you lifting up? Maybe you cared about something at some point, when you were struggling, but as soon as you got a foothold, as soon as your own rights were taken care of, you just –

> *(Making a "swhoomp" sound and gesture.)*

Out the window.

> *(She's spilled some of her drink making this gesture.)*

"Will and Grace," Supreme Court –

> *(Again she makes the swhoomp gesture.)*

Out the window.

*(She's spilled her drink again. **HENRY** takes it from her.)*

HENRY. I'm cutting you off

MYNA. Why, because I'm expressing myself?

HENRY. You're embarrassing yourself.

MYNA. Misogynist.

HENRY. Infant.

(Silence.)

MYNA. Give me the keys

HENRY. No

MYNA. Give me the keys to the car I'm not drunk I want the keys

HENRY. This is –

(Giving her the car keys.)

What did I even –?

MYNA. I feel <u>sorry</u> for you.
*(She looks at **JULES**.)* And you.
*(To **EZRA**.)* And you.

*(**MYNA** starts to storm out.)*

EZRA. *(To **CHRIS** and **PAM**.)* She doesn't feel sorry for you two.

MYNA. *(On her way out, not looking back.)* Thank you for having me, Pam, I had a lovely time.

*(The door slams. **HENRY** has locked eyes with **JULES**: does **MYNA** know?)*

HENRY. Myna!

(He goes after her.)

(Offstage.) Myna, wait! Jesus!

(Beat, beat.)

EZRA. *(Dry.)* Cute couple.

CHRIS. *Ezra.*

EZRA. What?

CHRIS. *(Suddenly on the verge of tears.)* Can *something* go without commentary? Without annotated bitchiness? Can anything just be allowed to – happen? With dignity?

(**CHRIS** *runs off.*)

EZRA. I have a joke about dignity but I'm gonna hold onto it.

PAM. Please do.

(**CHRIS** *comes back on, just as quickly.*)

CHRIS. Why weren't you on my side?

EZRA. I'm always on your side –

CHRIS. With the whole stupid / Elphaba –

EZRA. Because I didn't want it to turn into a whole thing with Henry again

CHRIS. You mean a race thing? Is that what you mean?

EZRA. Into a whatever thing, a whole culture wars thing. I wanted it all to go well

CHRIS. *(Biting.)* Right, Ezra the peacemaker.

EZRA. What does that mean?

CHRIS. Do you have any idea how often I don't get to have feelings? How I bite my tongue, when you run right over me while I'm telling a story, or you shut me down for even raising the idea of kids, when you know, you *know* / that it's –

EZRA. Right, because look around you, kids clearly equal happiness.

PAM. *(Serious.)* Watch it.

CHRIS. Ezra, I am ALWAYS the one who has to...

EZRA. What?

CHRIS. Make SPACE for you.

(**CHRIS** *starts to exit again.*)

EZRA. You're not really mad?

(**CHRIS** *slaps the cheese tray on his way out and the crackers go flying. He's gone.*)

(To himself.) Okay you are.

> *(***EZRA*** *looks at* ***PAM***. *She looks back. Is he going to go after* ***CHRIS***? *Instead he tosses back the rest of his drink.)*

PAM. I'm not sure I understand how this all...

EZRA. *(Wry.)* Yeah, we just started drinking.

PAM. Hon?

> *(***JULES*** *still isn't talking. It's weird.* ***PAM*** *moves toward her.)*

Is everything –?

JULES. Don't.

PAM. What?

JULES. I don't deserve it.

> *(A weird little pause.)*

I need a cigarette.

> *(***JULES*** *goes to the window and climbs out onto the deck.)*

> *(Sound of the baby crying in the monitor.)*

PAM. *(To no one in particular.)* I'll check on him.

> *(She goes.)*

> *(***EZRA*** *sits there for a minute, suddenly alone.)*

> *(He eyes the wrapped present that* ***HENRY*** *and* ***MYNA*** *brought. He opens it impulsively. It's a rubber ducky.)*

EZRA. *(Quietly appreciative.)* Classic.

Scene Ten

(**PAM** *stands in the baby's room. The* **BABY** *sits on the floor, just outside the tepee.*)

BABY. I couldn't sleep.

PAM. I'm sorry.

BABY. Do grown-ups have trouble sleeping?

PAM. That is one of the chief symptoms of being a grown-up.

(*She sits on the floor with him.*)

BABY. What do *you* do about it?

PAM. Sometimes I count sheep.

BABY. I've heard of that, but it seems asinine.

PAM. No, it actually works! You literally bore yourself to sleep. By the time I get to seventy I'm out.

BABY. I can't count that high.

(*Beat.*)

PAM. Don't you think you'll ever talk, baby?

(*Shorter beat.*)

I pretend not to worry, for your mom's sake.

BABY. Julia does worry.

PAM. You should call her Mom.

BABY. Does it suit her, though?

(*Beat.*)

PAM. I'm starting to imagine you can talk, to fill the void.

BABY. I can see that.

PAM. ... To keep myself company.

BABY. It's a dangerous road to go down. Julia would know. Sorry – "Mom."

PAM. I need someone to tell things to. Things like, I'm not sure I like our friends. They come here and give you a pat on the head and forget all about you. Maybe that's why you still can't talk.

(Beat.)

I could tell you a story, a sleepytime story.

BABY. Or: I could tell *you* a story.

PAM. You tell me?

BABY. I think you might already know it: my mom was in here with someone.

PAM. –

BABY. I didn't see, but I heard. Mom was here but she left her body. She was here and then she wasn't. And the stranger watched. And I watched the arrows on the side of the tepee. I can make them fly, with my mind, if I look hard enough.

PAM. Is this something you made up?

BABY. *(Placid.)* I don't think so.

> *(The door opens, **EZRA** peeks his head in. From this point on, the baby is silent.)*

EZRA. Can I come in?

PAM. *("You never come in here.")* Ezra?

EZRA. I got lonely.

PAM. Come sit with us.

EZRA. *(Sotto voce.)* I opened his present.

PAM. You opened –?

EZRA. Hartley's present. I needed to open something, it's a rubber ducky, I'm sorry.

PAM. Okay that's weird, but okay. He doesn't really understand wrapping things yet.

EZRA. I'm sorry.

> *(**EZRA** sits on the floor with them.)*

PAM. Hartley, you remember your uncle Ezra.

BABY. –

EZRA. Maybe not, I've been kind of a deadbeat uncle.

PAM. He remembers.

EZRA. I'm not even your uncle really, it's kind of an honorary thing, but. Good to see you.

PAM. Is Jules?

EZRA. Still smoking.

>   *(Beat.)*

Does he wanna play a game or something?

PAM. I think he's tuckered out.

>   *(Mini-beat.)*

It's nice sometimes, to sit in silence with your child.

EZRA. Chris wants a child.

PAM. I know.

EZRA. He wants it so much I can't bear it.

He tries to pretend but he's bad at pretending.

PAM. He really is.

>   *(They look at the **BABY**. Maybe the **BABY** burps.)*

It's a lot of work.

EZRA. Still. He's beautiful.

PAM. Is he?

I can't tell anymore.

>   *(They sit with the **BABY**, sad and quiet, as the light fades.)*

Scene Eleven

*(Late that night. **CHRIS** lies in bed, unable to sleep, thoughts racing.)*

(Suddenly, a sound like distant gunfire. He sits up, scared. Turns on the bedside lamp.)

CHRIS. What was that?

Ezra?

*(**CHRIS** sees that **EZRA**'s side of the bed is empty.)*

Ezra?

*(From the shadows, the distinguished **VOICE** of an unseen figure.)*

VOICE. There's no time to find your friend. The day we feared has arrived.

CHRIS. *(?)* The day –

VOICE. The Anschluss, you little fool. We must away at once.

CHRIS. Away to where?

*(Light rises, and we see that the unseen figure looks an awful lot like **CAPTAIN VON TRAPP**. He fills out his Austrian military uniform very nicely.)*

*(He is played by the actor who plays **EZRA**, convincingly butch.)*

CAPTAIN VON TRAPP. Across the Alps, of course. Our poor old world is crumbling.

CHRIS. *(Starting to get into the groove.)* Will it be far?

CAPTAIN VON TRAPP. It will be as far as our voices are strong.

CHRIS. *(Trying to parse that.)* So "uh-oh" but also "yay"?

*(**CAPTAIN VON TRAPP** blows his whistle.)*

CHRIS. ?

> (**CAPTAIN VON TRAPP** *blows his whistle again.*)

I don't know what that means.

> (**CAPTAIN VON TRAPP** *climbs into bed with him.*)

Oh, I think I see.

> (**CAPTAIN VON TRAPP** *does a more complicated whistle. He glances down towards the covers.*)

Yes, Captain.

CAPTAIN VON TRAPP. *(Softly.)* We must be very quiet, or the Nazis will hear us.

> (**CHRIS** *disappears under the covers.*)

> (**CAPTAIN VON TRAPP** *closes his eyes, focused on the sensation.*)

Good lad.

> (*He turns out the bedside lamp. In the darkness.*)

CHRIS'S VOICE. *(Softly.)* Yeah. Wanna be good.

EZRA'S VOICE. Chris?

Are you masturbating?

> (*Suddenly* **EZRA** *turns on the bedside lamp.*)

CHRIS. What? No!

EZRA. Are you masturbating about Nazis?

CHRIS. No –

EZRA. ...While I'm sleeping?

CHRIS. No!

EZRA. You were! I heard you!

CHRIS. But you were there too! It was you, only you were Captain Von Trapp!

EZRA. As played by Christopher Plummer or Stephen Moyer?

CHRIS. *(Obviously.)* Christopher Plummer!

EZRA. But why the Nazis?

CHRIS. They were ancillary!

(*Beat.*)

EZRA. Did I look good?

CHRIS. *(Yes.)* I mean, it was working for me.

EZRA. Well. Thank you.

(*Beat.*)

EZRA. I have some knee-high boots in the closet somewhere, if you want to really

CHRIS. Ha

EZRA. Go there.

(*Mini-beat.*)

CHRIS. Why do you have knee-high boots?

EZRA. I was Captain Morgan for Halloween one year.

CHRIS. That's a really weird costume.

EZRA. My friend was Johnny Walker, and his boyfriend was the Guinness Toucan. It was, what's it called, anthological.

(*A beat, then.*)

That was crazy, today.

CHRIS. Yes

EZRA. I hope Henry's okay.

CHRIS. I hope that *girl's* okay.

(*Little beat.*)

EZRA. I hope *you're* okay.

CHRIS. Thank you.

EZRA. That was – I'll do better.

(*A kiss.*)

I was thinking.

If it really means a lot to you

I was thinking

We could have a discussion, at least

CHRIS. *(?)* A discussion

EZRA. About whether – oh my god, this sucks – about whether it would be totally crazy for us to maybe have a kid.

>   *(Beat.)*

CHRIS. *(With sudden feeling: "Do you mean it?")* Ezra?

EZRA. Call me Captain.

Scene Twelve

(A month later. **CHRIS** *and* **EZRA** *sit with* **HENRY** *in a bar. Whiskeys and longnecks.)*

EZRA. So you're my oldest friend, right?

HENRY. I knew Lisa Schwank in grade school.

EZRA. You knew me in grade school.

HENRY. By reputation. *(To* **CHRIS**.*)* The limpest wrist in the fourth grade.

*(***CHRIS** *chuckles.)*

EZRA. Ha ha, Ezra is effeminate, that's not the point.

The point is we are talking about having a kid, me and Chris, / and we

HENRY. I thought you didn't / want to –

EZRA. And now we do, and we've been looking into options, surrogates

CHRIS. Four year adoption waits

EZRA. And finally we thought – hey – we want a kid, and Henry wants a kid, and I know this is borderline insane but maybe we could all have a kid together. Joy, tears. Christmas, Hannukah.

(Beat.)

Well, what do you think? Good idea?

HENRY. It's a good idea in the sense that it makes me laugh.

CHRIS. You're not laughing

EZRA. You could at least think about it

CHRIS. He doesn't want to, Ezra. *(To* **HENRY**.*)* Never mind, this was stupid.

EZRA. *(Defensive, to* **CHRIS**.*)* It was your idea.

*(***HENRY** *looks at* **CHRIS**.*)*

We just thought, since Myna is no longer um

CHRIS. Ezra

EZRA. ...A *factor*, not that she sounded very enthusiastic.

HENRY. Do you mean we would all adopt one kid and like share the visitation or – what do you mean?

EZRA. No, silly. You would have it. You.

> (**EZRA** *quickly mimes the curve of a pregnant belly.)*
>
> *(Beat.)*
>
> *(Then, quietly.)*

HENRY. Oh.

> *(Beat.)*

EZRA. Are you happy or sad? I can't tell.
   (To **CHRIS.***)* Is he happy or sad?

HENRY. *(Irritated.)* Are those my only options?

EZRA. We wouldn't have to have sex of course

HENRY. *(Fake-disappointed.)* Aw, no?

EZRA. Vials and beakers, purely antiseptic.

CHRIS. *("Ew.")* Beakers

EZRA. Or however it works.

> *(Beat.* **HENRY** *is still regaining his footing. Confused and highly skeptical.)*

HENRY. Why your sperm?

EZRA. Why my / sperm –?

HENRY. Not Chris's. You just assumed it would be yours?

CHRIS. His sperm count is better.

> (**EZRA** *gestures like "I'm the champion of the world.")*

Plus it makes my eggs drop a little thinking of a mini-Ezra running around the playground. I know, there's something wrong with me.

HENRY. *(Quiet, inward.)* This isn't –.
   I wanted to be one thing.
   I didn't want to be in between.

EZRA. You mean

HENRY. Some people like being "they."

They like in between, none of the above.

I wanted to be "him."

I worked so hard.

EZRA. Why does this make you not a him?

(The color drains from **HENRY***'s face.)*

HENRY. *(Stark.)* Do you know anything about me?

EZRA. Uh

HENRY. Do you want to know? Do you care?

EZRA. Yes, I care, yes!

HENRY. Because it kind of feels like you have no idea what you're asking me.

CHRIS. To go off hormones.

HENRY. That is not a –

Easy –.

CHRIS. We know.

HENRY. I waited two years to look like this –

On top of all the years it took me to figure out I didn't look like who I was.

Two years of crazy acne, and night sweats, and mood swings

And wanting to fuck everything that stands

Two years

To walk into a men's room without getting a look.

To get "sirred" by a hot girl

Now everyone says "sir"

Everyone

Stewardesses, kids

So it's not nothing.

EZRA. No.

(Longer beat.)

HENRY. *(Still very much not on board.)* How would we even – half the time at your place, half at mine?

CHRIS. Or we all get one big place, you're downstairs, we're upstairs –

EZRA. *("Maybe not that.")* We'd figure it out.

> *(Little beat.)*

HENRY. Do we even like each other anymore?

EZRA. What? Of course we do!

HENRY. Sometimes I can't tell.

> *(Little beat. Then to **CHRIS**.)*

And have we even / seen each other –

CHRIS. No we have not   ,

HENRY. – Since?

CHRIS. *(Choosing to be diplomatic.)* I blame the mojitos.

HENRY. I wasn't drinking mojitos.

> *(Beat. That had the faintest whiff of an apology from **HENRY**.)*

I thought we were here to like bury the hatchet, not plan the next twenty years of our lives.

EZRA. Exactly, though. The fact that we're here, asking you to go on this ride with us?

Everyone fights, Chris and I fight. If we didn't care, we wouldn't fight.

> *(There's a kind of wan aftertaste to this.)*

HENRY. It's not good enough, is it.

EZRA. What do you want me to say? I love you, Henry. It's different than it was. Our relationship – changed. I don't know if it's my fault or your fault.

> *(A quick amendment, off of **HENRY**'s steely expression.)*

Okay not your fault. I don't know how this –. My whole life it's "Smear the Queer" and getting slammed into lockers, and then I wake up and I'm Mr. Mainstream Privilege. I didn't see it happening. I'm sorry.

> *(A beat, then.)*

HENRY. Thank you.

EZRA. *(Prompting* **HENRY** *and* **CHRIS**.*)* "No Ezra, you're not Mr. Mainstream Privilege..."

(**HENRY** *and* **CHRIS** *are silent.)*

'Nother round?

HENRY. Please.

CHRIS. Yeah.

(**EZRA** *exits to get their drinks. Beat, then.)*

HENRY. It was your idea?

CHRIS. I like it being someone we know.

(Little beat.)

HENRY. Is it hopeless?

CHRIS. Is what / hopeless

HENRY. Sorry. I mean, your sperm count.
It's just, I've known Ezra so long that it's...

CHRIS. Weird.

(**HENRY** *nods. They both look in the direction* **EZRA** *exited.)*

HENRY. Plus, you're taller.

(**CHRIS** *smiles.)*

Scene Thirteen

(A year later. 2016 now, for those keeping track. **JULES** *and* **PAM**'s *place.* **EZRA** *is there with a very pregnant* **HENRY**.)

(Somewhere in the room, there is a mylar balloon in the shape of a bald eagle. Stars and stripes.)

EZRA. So we wait for the martinis to arrive first.

JULES. Since that worked out so well last time.

EZRA. Right? And I take a big gulp, and tell him:
Dad, you're gonna be a grandfather. And he just sits there

PAM. Oh god

EZRA. For I swear five minutes of silence, before he finally says, "I don't get it. You knocked up Helen?"

HENRY. He's still dead-naming me. *(Shudder.)* Helen. The name itself is...

EZRA. Insurmountable.

JULES. Well, Helen Mirren.

PAM. That's not helpful, honey

JULES. Helen Keller. It wasn't the *greatest* obstacle she faced.

HENRY. Fair

EZRA. *(To* **JULES**.) This is not

JULES. Sorry

EZRA. ... Germaine. So my dad says, "You got your friend Helen knocked up? Does that mean you're both straight again?" And I say, "Yes, Dad. You were right all along, it *was* just a phase. Helen is growing her hair back and I'm gonna get some pleated, whatever, khakis."

PAM. *(Setting down a cheese plate.)* Crackers.

EZRA. "No, Dad. Chris and I wanted a baby, and Henry (who is a man and always *has* been a man) wanted a baby, and Henry's eggs and Chris's sperm played well together, so yay."

HENRY. And Ezra's dad says

EZRA. Long pause long pause

HENRY. "I remember when that poor Ryan White got sick."

JULES. You're fucking with us.

EZRA. No

PAM. Again?

EZRA. "When that poor kid got sick, that's when people started to pay attention. It wasn't just the gays in the big cities anymore. You people have a lot to thank him for."

JULES. When is it ever a good idea to say "you people."

EZRA. And I say Dad: There is going to be a *baby*.

The baby is your grandson.

We are not talking about hemophiliacs or lesions or dead gay people Dad so

Please

Stop associating joyous landmark occasions in the life of your son who happens to be gay with with with death and disease and Ryan White, Dad please.

And he just says

JULES. I'm scared

EZRA. "Will the kid be a trans person?"

> *(They look at **HENRY**'s pregnant belly.)*

And Henry is like:

HENRY. "We're gonna try."

> *(**PAM** snorts.)*

"If it's a boy, we'll get pink sheets and a doll. If it's a girl, blue sheets and some chewing tobacco. We should be able to confuse it pretty good before long."

> *(Beat.)*

EZRA. Should we turn on the TV? Everyone's saying it's going to be over by 6:30.

JULES. I get too nervous

EZRA. *("Don't be nervous.")* Huffington Post has her at ninety-seven percent.

JULES. Huffington Post is a rag.

PAM. They'll never call it before eight o'clock – they're all too cautious about pulling a Dewey defeats Truman.

EZRA. *(Did I stutter?)* <u>Ninety-seven</u> percent.

HENRY. I hope he loses every state.

> *(Beat.)*

EZRA. How's Hartley? Is he...?

> *(**JULES** looks at **PAM**. Then she just shakes her head. Difficult.)*

Soon.

PAM. *(To **HENRY**.)* Is the nausea over?

HENRY. Mostly. There's a lingering need for pickles.

PAM. Do you feel at all – I don't know how to say this – maternal?

HENRY. My hips are back. My big stupid hips. So that's a drag. For the first few months I could pass as a fat Midwestern guy, but now it's like

> *(Delineating his wide hips.)*

"Hello."

PAM. But emotionally I mean, / do you feel –

HENRY. Oh yeah, I'm all over the place. But it was like that on T too. Of course this whole thing has pretty much fucked over my sex drive, but maybe pregnant women have that too

JULES. Pam was a minx when she was pregnant

PAM. I wasn't

JULES. A dirty minx.

PAM. If you say so.

> *(Beat.)*

HENRY. I get looks.

People don't offer me a seat on the subway. They don't pat my tummy like it's magic.

JULES. *There's* a plus.

HENRY. *(Re:* **EZRA**.*)* And, I get to make this guy wait on me hand and foot.

EZRA. At your service, my liege

HENRY. But it's hard. I mean look at me. I used to be this playah.

(This hangs in the air. **JULES** *looks away.)*

PAM. Well. Only three more months.

JULES. How is Chris?

PAM. Jules –

JULES. *(To* **PAM**.*)* Are we supposed to not talk about him? At all?

EZRA. That was the plan.

JULES. We don't even know what happened. He's our friend too.

*(***EZRA*** *looks at* **HENRY**. **HENRY** *shrugs.)*

EZRA. Um. So this is six weeks ago. Chris was coming back from the trip to Boston, so I was cooking this fancy, like, Spanish thing from the *Times* website. *Fideos*. Romantic. And he texts from the airport that he's landed so I – I'm looking out the window for him, nervous fellow that I am. And I put the fideos in the oven to crisp, and now I have a little time, I pour a glass of wine, and I look out the window again and there's a cab there, a way's down the street, just parked there with its off duty light on and – hmm that's odd – this cab taking a break on this little brownstone street. And I look a little closer and I see that the guy, the cabbie's head is tilted back in the front seat, like

(He tilts his head back, using the crook of his arm as a pillow.)

EZRA. And I realize this dude is getting a blowjob, good for him, he's really getting into it, really face-fucking whoever it is.

PAM. Oh no

EZRA. And I'm thinking maybe I'll take a picture, I'll Instagram it. Funny. And I look away for a second to get my phone and when I look again...

PAM. Chris.

EZRA. It's Chris, in the front seat of this cab, parked on our street. It's Chris who's been giving this middle-aged fucking *Saudi* guy / or whatever

HENRY. *("Settle down.")* Hey

EZRA. ... The blow job of his fucking life. On our street. Like he must've said to the guy, "Go a little farther, past our house, that way he won't see. My husband won't see."

> *(Beat.)*

JULES. That's the foulest thing I've ever heard.

> *(**PAM** looks at her.)*

EZRA. And of course Henry was already pregnant. All of this was already –

JULES. Some people can't let themselves be happy. They have to just – burn it all.

PAM. I think that's true.

> *(**PAM** directs this at **JULES**. **JULES** breaks eye contact.)*

HENRY. It'll still be Chris's baby, of course.

PAM. Of course.

JULES. How will that work?

HENRY. We'll make it.

PAM. *(To **EZRA**.)* I mean Chris was the whole reason, right?

EZRA. *(The phrase turns into something larger in his mouth.)* He was. He was the whole reason.

PAM. Has he tried to / make amends?

EZRA. He's tried

PAM. And you won't even consider?

JULES. Did you not just hear the story?

PAM. Sometimes you have to forgive people.

(*Again, we sense this is for* **JULES**.)

Not just for them, but for you.

HENRY. That's what I keep telling him! There are gay couples who wouldn't blink at a stray blowjob here and there.

EZRA. Yeah, well, not us.

HENRY. They put it in their wedding vows, "For better or worse, except when Idris Elba is in town."

EZRA. And that is fine for *those people*, but I am a rare and apparently endangered species of person who wants someone who doesn't sneak around / and lie –

PAM. But eight years together. Surely there's a / way to –

EZRA. I don't think so.

(*Pause.* **HENRY** *squeezes* **EZRA***'s shoulder.*)

Look at us, reenacting our fucking prom photo.
The homo who asked the lesbian to the prom – here we are, twenty years later, American Gothic.

HENRY. We were always on the edge of not being friends anymore / and now –

EZRA. Totally

HENRY. We're like buddies who've been through a war together.

JULES. Did you ever think, maybe you could be something more?

(*Beat.*)

EZRA. Jules, that is so –

PAM.	**HENRY.**
Yeah, honey	Gross

JULES. What?

EZRA. Are you auditioning for the role of my father? What exactly about our collective experiences and genitals makes you think that would be a banner idea? That's like saying, "Jules, why don't <u>you</u> and Henry have a thing?" The math isn't even right.

(**PAM** *goes and pours herself a glass of water.*)

JULES. It wasn't a *recommendation*. It was just a light musing: maybe there's a real family here, right under your noses, and you're not realizing.

EZRA. Um

HENRY. It <u>is</u> a real family.

JULES. Of course.

PAM. No one's eating. Try the Point Reyes Blue, it's really nice.

(*Little beat.*)

JULES. It's funny, that you'll be reminded.
When you look at the baby.

(**PAM** *puts her head in her hands.*)

EZRA. (*To* **JULES.**) You mean because he'll be half-black?

PAM. (*To* **JULES.**) What are you doing?

JULES. (*To* **EZRA.**) I meant because he'll look like Chris.

HENRY. That's not what you / meant.

PAM. (*To* **JULES.**) Is this some kind of social experiment?

JULES. (*Defensive.*) The baby will be half-black, yes, on a playground with two white parents, and maybe people will think he's adopted, and you will tell them no, he's not adopted, and what you won't tell them is that his biological father royally fucked you over and is now out of the picture. I'm sorry if it's politically incorrect to point that out. I thought you wanted to throw off the chains of our PC oppressors.

EZRA. Not when it comes to my fucking kid.

JULES. I'm sorry, (*Then to* **HENRY.**) Sorry. This is all very...

HENRY. (*Yes.*) This is all very.

(Beat.)

PAM. Honey, why don't you go show Henry those hand-me-downs.

HENRY. Oh, I'm sure they'll be great. We'll be grateful to get whatever.

PAM. *(A command.)* Honey, I really think you should show him.

EZRA. What's going on

JULES. *(To HENRY.)* Come on. She's giving me her scary Gordon Gekko look.

(JULES and HENRY exit.)

PAM. Hi.

EZRA. Hi?

PAM. I know we aren't friends the way you and my wife are –

EZRA. That's not true –

PAM. But I think in this case I bring more clarity to the issue. I think you're making a mistake.

EZRA. Sorry?

PAM. Actually there's no "think." You are making a mistake.

EZRA. *(Rising.)* Look, Pam –

PAM. Sit.

(He does.)

EZRA. *(Under his breath, à la Nora.)* "Sit down, Torvald."

PAM. *(Ignoring this.)* You found someone to share your life with. You can stand him every day, and he can stand you. These are things some people never find. You're going to have a child. <u>So</u> he put a man's penis in his mouth.

EZRA. *("That didn't sound so hot.")* Oof you really are a lesbian

PAM. *(Powering through.)* Maybe it's happened before, maybe it will happen again. You have every right to be outraged and hurt and betrayed. But is it worth giving up everything?

EZRA. I'm not giving it up, / he took it –

PAM. Except you are, because you're the one who can make it go away. My advice? Let go of whatever Hollywood version you have in your head of how this is supposed to go. Sit down with Chris. Make some coffee. Come up with something that works for you. Maybe Chris gets to suck a cock each month. Maybe he has to scrub the apartment every time as penance. He has to put a dollar in the cock jar.

EZRA. If you're gonna be glib / about this –

PAM. Maybe he goes to a therapist, for sex addiction.

Or you make him promise never again, and you choose to believe him.

EZRA. That sounds...better.

> *(Little beat.)*

PAM. It's not.

EZRA. What do you mean?

PAM. Because you'll never be done. Choosing to believe.

You have to keep choosing every day.

The really fun part is you're gonna have to listen to what he wants too. He might say you have to put out a little more –

EZRA. Right, because blame the victim

PAM. He might want to bring people over, sometimes, as long as it includes you –

EZRA. I don't *want* to be included, Pam! I want a *marriage*, not some bargain-basement model filled with exception clauses –

PAM. Escape clauses –

EZRA. Yeah, that. I want a real marriage, not some low-cal version the gays cooked up so they could still fool around at the White Party.

PAM. This is real marriage. This is what straight people have been doing for thousands of years. You marry someone, you make promises, then you find out they're a little different than you thought. Or *you're* a little different than you thought. And you try to keep the thing from dying. Don't you think my grandmother in the '50s caught my grandfather with a dick in his mouth a few times? Or not a dick, but –

EZRA. Maybe.

PAM. Actually now that I think about it, maybe.

> *(Beat. A feeling that her words are finally sinking in.)*

EZRA. I hate this.

PAM. At least Chris picked some stranger, not someone you have to see every day.

> *(Beat.* **EZRA** *looks to the door where* **JULES** *and* **HENRY** *exited. Has he figured it out?)*

EZRA. You mean –

PAM. Just make sure that these new rules, whatever they are, they are yours – yours and his – they're new wedding vows, in a way.

I love you, Ezra, but you are a lot, I mean you are a LOT. And if Chris can do eight years of it and survive, then, well.

> *(She makes a gesture like, "You get it." Pause.)*

EZRA. That is literally the most you've ever talked.

PAM. Yes.

EZRA. Aha. Back to monosyllables.

PAM. We'll see.

JULES. *(From offstage, quiet dread.)* Oh god. Oh god.

PAM. Honey? Are you okay?

> *(***JULES** *re-enters, looking at her phone, very disturbed. Followed by* **HENRY***.)*

JULES. It's over

HENRY. Don't be crazy, they haven't counted half of Florida

JULES. It's over

PAM. What's going on?

JULES. Turn on the TV.

(Lights.)

Scene Fourteen

(Several months later. 2017 now. **HENRY'S BABY***, played by the actor who plays* **CHRIS***, sits with* **JULES'S BABY***. Like the other baby,* **HENRY'S BABY** *is pensive, blunt. Not at all cutesy.)*

(Stuffed animals and handcrafted wood toys abound. **JULES'S BABY** *holds a balloon shaped like a big green number "4.")*

HENRY'S BABY. Balloon.

JULES'S BABY. Not their best effort.

HENRY'S BABY. I like it. Green.

JULES'S BABY. *(Dismissive.)* Babies like everything.

HENRY'S BABY. You're not that much older.

JULES'S BABY. *("Old.")* Four. The beginning of socialization, the concept of sharing

HENRY'S BABY. What's sharing?

JULES'S BABY. Exactly.

HENRY'S BABY. *(Grabbing for the balloon.)* I want to hold it. Let me hold it.

JULES'S BABY. I would if I could...

*(***JULES'S BABY** *lets the balloon go.)*

HENRY'S BABY. No!

JULES'S BABY. I'm still learning the particulars of sharing.

(They watch it float up to the ceiling.)

I think I might be bored.

HENRY'S BABY. Oh?

JULES'S BABY. Mom said only boring people get bored, but Other Mom said fascinating people are the *most* bored. Gertrude Stein, she said. Truman Capote. The world isn't clever enough to surprise them. Sometimes they kill themselves 'cause at least that'll be different. George Sanders, Marilyn Monroe.

HENRY'S BABY. Did she kill herself really?

JULES'S BABY. *(Sage.)* There are many theories.

>   *(Beat.)*

I could tell you a story.

HENRY'S BABY. Is it a scary story?

JULES'S BABY. *(Hard to answer.)* It depends how you respond to the truth.

HENRY'S BABY. Are there monsters in it?

JULES'S BABY. It depends how you define "monsters."

HENRY'S BABY. You're not telling me much about this story, but okay.

JULES'S BABY. There was a girl and a girl –

HENRY'S BABY. *(A correction.)* Once upon a time.

JULES'S BABY. Once upon a time, there was a girl and a girl. And, a boy and a boy. And they were all of them friends.

HENRY'S BABY. Were there babies?

JULES'S BABY. There were no babies – not yet. Good question. And, as a result, they did a great many things. They went out to supper, and ate foods that were different colors and sizes. And saw shows, which are like stories acted out. And they drank a kind of potion that made them feel more smart and beautiful, at least in moderation.

HENRY'S BABY. *(Sounds delicious.)* Mm.

JULES'S BABY. So that was all very nice. But the strange thing was, the other people in the world had paired off differently

HENRY'S BABY. *(?)* Differently.

JULES'S BABY. Boy and girl. Girl and boy.

HENRY'S BABY. Curious

JULES'S BABY. Isn't it

HENRY'S BABY. The potential for confusion –

JULES'S BABY. Yes

HENRY'S BABY. ...For mistranslation – from boy language to girl, and back again.

JULES'S BABY. Nevertheless, it was the thing to do. The norm. And a kind of law was passed to say that the girl and girl, and the boy and boy, did not *really* love each other, not in the same way – they were just good friends.

HENRY'S BABY. Is this the scary part?

JULES'S BABY. Not really, not yet. Because in no time at all, the law was gone.

HENRY'S BABY. And happy ever after?

JULES'S BABY. Hardly. Because then another sort of pair came along. New sorts of pairs. And they weren't boy and girl exactly. Or they weren't but also they were.

HENRY'S BABY. I don't understand

JULES'S BABY. Neither did anyone else. The words themselves broke. Boy. Girl. Suddenly they seemed insufficient. People needed more words, but no one could agree on what the new words should be.

HENRY'S BABY. *(Suggestions.)* "Rumpet." "Bunce." "Kevinteen."

JULES'S BABY. *("No.")* Those are new words.

HENRY'S BABY. I'm only trying to help.

JULES'S BABY. And what was odd is that our heroes, the boy and boy, and the girl and girl, they didn't welcome these new pairs. They'd forgotten what it was like to not be welcome.

HENRY'S BABY. Why?

JULES'S BABY. *("Exactly.")* Yes, why.
But then something happened, and they remembered.
Something awful happened and the floor fell away.
And the boy and the boy, and the girl and the girl, were reminded how far there was to go.

　　　(Beat.)

HENRY'S BABY. I'm not sure I like this story.

JULES'S BABY. Why not?

HENRY'S BABY. I want one with a happy ending. Like, "Then they all ate ice cream." Or, "They rescued the green balloon from the ceiling and it became their friend."

JULES'S BABY. We won't know the ending for a long time. So much has to happen first.

HENRY'S BABY. Like what?

JULES'S BABY. We have to grow up, you and me
And have kids of our own maybe.
What will be normal by the time we're grown up? By the time we're very old? What is normal that we don't know is normal? What are our minds still too small to understand?
I get a little overwhelmed.

> (*Beat. A sudden clarity for* **HENRY'S BABY**.)

HENRY'S BABY. Is that why you don't talk?

JULES'S BABY. You mean –

HENRY'S BABY. If you don't talk, none of it has to begin. You'll stay in your room, and the balloons will come once a year, and nothing will change.

JULES'S BABY. And I'll be perfect. I won't say the wrong thing, the way they do.

HENRY'S BABY. (*A kind of challenge.*) And there'll be no story.

> (**JULES'S BABY** *looks at* **HENRY'S BABY**.)

> (**JULES'S BABY** *looks at the baby monitor.*)

I know, it's scary. The beginning.

> (*Lights snap to* **JULES** *and* **PAM** *in the living room with* **EZRA**. *Everyone has drinks.*)

EZRA. And then I did the voice of the crocodile like it was Paul Lynde and the ladybug was Samantha from *Sex and the City*, but dialed up a few notches.

JULES. (*Is that possible?*) Dialed *up*?

EZRA. Mm-hmm. So I'm the storytime guy and then Henry takes over. He's the one with the touch.

JULES. *(?)* The touch

EZRA. The ability to induce sleep with a mere bouncy dance.

PAM. Swaying is very important.

JULES. I wish someone would sway *me* these days

PAM. She hasn't been sleeping

JULES. Can anyone?

CHRIS. *(Offstage.)* Hey babe?

> (**CHRIS** *appears in the window, the one that leads to the roof deck, with barbecue tongs and a chef's apron.* **HENRY** *is out on the deck with him.)*

Can you maybe come look at the coals? I feel like they're ready. God. I don't know why I'm the designated butch.

JULES. 'Specially when my wife is here.

PAM. Ha ha.

EZRA. *(Finishing his drink.)* One more / swig.

> *(Suddenly, over the baby monitor, we hear a child's voice.)*

> *(A real four year old, for the first time.)*

HARTLEY'S VOICE. Ma

> *(**JULES** looks at **PAM**.)*

JULES. Am I hallucinating?

Or / did you?

PAM. No I think I heard it too

HENRY. I did

EZRA. What? I didn't hear / anything –

JULES. Shut up, shut up, he'll do it again

EZRA. Don't tell me to / shut up

JULES. Ezra, I love you, shut up!

> *(They all wait.)*

> *(A short but endless pause, then.)*

HARTLEY'S VOICE. Ma.

> (**JULES** *jumps to her feet. Mouth open wide,*
> *eyes darting with unprocessable joy.*)

Ma Ma Ma Ma Ma Ma Ma Ma Ma Ma Ma Ma Ma Ma
Ma-ma.

JULES. "Mama."

PAM. That's us.

JULES. That's us.

> (*Lights.*)

End of Play

AUTHOR'S NOTE & APPENDIX

There is a word in this play that I didn't think I would ever type. I want to share the story of how it came to be in the script.

In Scene Seven, there is a passage that originally read as follows:

CHRIS. You're putting me in a category with all the high school fucktards I had to grow up with in Wichita. The ones who played lacrosse and dated cheerleaders and dressed up in their cheerleader girlfriends' outfits on Halloween for fun, who felt at home in their own skin, who called me faggot. Or worse.

In the premiere production at Playwrights Horizons, Chris was played by the actor Phillip James Brannon, who has a sharp and generous dramaturgical brain. About a week into rehearsal, Phillip came to me at the end of the day to discuss the above speech. He said, "If it was me, I would just say it. I would just say 'nigger.' I'm not afraid of that word. White people are afraid of that word." I couldn't argue with that. But I remained reticent about whether it was my right to put the word in a play – even if it was in the mouth of a black character, and even if the black actor playing him had suggested it.

It was a good week before I finally revised the scene into the version that appears in this acting edition. Because of course, it wasn't just a matter of adding the word. It changed the temperature of the room, both on stage and off; it changed how we heard everything that followed in the scene. For me, the breakthrough was adding Jules's incredulous reaction, "They really said that?" and Chris's dry response, "Yeah girl." The audience felt the permission to tentatively laugh again, observing the inability of the white characters to see their own privilege. In a play that is meant to be about difficult conversations, it felt wrong to withhold this bit of difficulty – and to deprive the character of Chris with the full force of his argument in a scene about who experienced the most marginalization.

I will leave others to discuss the boundaries of white writers scripting black characters. What I feel equipped to say, is that in this play, in this scene, for this actor, it was the right choice. For future productions, it seems to me that the choice should rest with the actor playing Chris. I am including the original version of the passage below, in case the actor finds it preferable.

> **CHRIS.** You're putting me in a category with all the high school fucktards I had to grow up with in Wichita. The ones who played lacrosse and dated cheerleaders and dressed up in their cheerleader girlfriends' outfits on Halloween for fun, who felt at home in their own skin, who called me faggot. / Or worse.
>
> **MYNA.** Oh, god
>
> **CHRIS.** *(Continuous.)* You're saying I'm one / of them
>
> **MYNA.** No we're not.
>
> **EZRA.** Well yes, actually. You're saying they're a cis guy and Chris and I are cis guys and all of us got the keys to the kingdom, and it didn't feel that way for the first three-decades-plus of our lives.
>
> **HENRY.** And now it does.
>
> **EZRA.** What?   **MYNA.** *("Steady.")* Henry.
>
> **HENRY.** You said yourself: You didn't feel that way for three decades, and now / you do –
>
> **EZRA.** I just mean how in the last couple years, things have gotten a little / more –
>
> **HENRY.** And for me it's still three more decades of public bathroom legislation, three more decades of driving to the fucking desert to find people who are like-minded, so yeah, I think you belong in a category of people who are currently easier for society to accept, and there is a name for that category and it is called a "cis male."

JULES. Maybe it's the word

HENRY. What?

JULES. Maybe the problem is the word sucks.

HENRY. Whoa.

JULES. Cis. I mean what does that even / mean –

MYNA. It's Latin / I think

HENRY. It means "on this side of," as opposed to the other / side

EZRA. Well it sounds like "siss," like S-I-S, / like sissy.

MYNA. It's C-I

EZRA. *(Continuous.)* I just don't see why the trans community gets to call us something that we were scared to get called in middle school.

HENRY. (shrug) Homonyms.

EZRA. So, you get to choose what we call you and what you call us.

HENRY. I'll call you what I want. No one's saying you have to answer.

*(**CHRIS** is shaking his head, still processing all this.)*

CHRIS. I'm sorry, but. You really think I have the keys to the kingdom?

HENRY. Those were Ezra's words –

CHRIS. That I have some sort of advantage, in this society, over a white trans guy?

HENRY. Maybe not every black cis guy, but your parents have money.

CHRIS. Oh, now we're / talking about

HENRY. You grew up in the biggest house in the whole state of Kansas – *(To **EZRA**.)* Didn't you / say that?

EZRA. One of the biggest, maybe

CHRIS. *(To **HENRY**.)* So I'm not black. Because I have a trust fund and a bunch of white / friends.

HENRY. I would never / say that

EZRA. *(To* **CHRIS.***)* He's not saying / that

HENRY. I'm just saying the challenges of someone with money and a Harvard diploma aren't the same as / someone who –

CHRIS. How does that help me when I walk into a store and the manager follows me around; when I try to get a cab. I'm a faggot in Harlem and I'm a "thug" in white Brooklyn. How is that cis? How is that "on this side of"? No matter where I am, it's the other side of.

> *(Pause pause pause.* **EZRA** *rubs* **CHRIS***'s shoulder.* **CHRIS** *shakes his hand off.)*

MYNA. Um, Ezra, what are you writing these days?